Aloha, Salty!

Aloha, Salty!

GLORIA RAND

illustrated by
TED RAND

HENRY HOLT AND COMPANY · NEW YORK

Henry Holt and Company, Inc.
Publishers since 1866
115 West 18th Street
New York, New York 10011

Published in Canada by Fitzhenry & Whiteside Ltd.,
195 Allstate Parkway, Markham, Ontario L3R 4T8.

Library of Congress Cataloging-in-Publication Data
Rand, Gloria.
Aloha, Salty! / by Gloria Rand; illustrated by Ted Rand.
Summary: Zack and Salty Dog run into a storm while sailing to Hawaii.
[1. Sailing—Fiction. 2. Storms—Fiction. 3. Dogs—Fiction.
4. Hawaii—Fiction.] I. Rand, Ted, ill. II. Title.
PZ7.R1553A1 1995 [E]—dc20   95-22845
ISBN 0-8050-3429-3
First Edition—1996
Printed in the United States of America
on acid-free paper. ∞
1 3 5 7 9 10 8 6 4 2

In memory of our family dog, Spike,
the original Salty Dog

Land ho! We'll be ashore tomorrow!"
Zack shouted to Salty Dog. "That's
Hawaii straight ahead." Zack pointed to a
tiny speck on the horizon. "Aloha,
Hawaii! Aloha from Zack and Salty!"

It had been several weeks since Zack and Salty set sail from Alaska. Day after day they had been at sea all by themselves, except when whales splashed and spouted nearby or porpoises swam alongside the boat. Sometimes gooney birds tried to land on deck and flying fish flopped themselves aboard. Never did a ship or even another boat come into view.

"Glad I've had you along, Old Salt." Zack patted his dog's head. "It would have been far too lonesome sailing across this big ocean by myself."

Salty wagged his tail as if to say he agreed.

Zack and Salty, like all good deep-sea sailors, wore life jackets whenever they were out on deck, and safety harnesses hooked onto the boat's lifeline at all times, when they were topside or down below. They ate well to stay strong, were careful not to get hurt, and never went swimming off the boat. Sharks often lurked nearby ready to attack.

During the whole voyage, Salty had been an excellent crew. When it was time to bucket down the deck, he got the mop. When their quarters needed cleaning, he shook out the rug. When Zack did the dishes, Salty was there with his own dirty bowl to have it washed too.

"We'll be taking on fresh water and adding supplies to our ship stores as soon as we get ashore," Zack told Salty. "We've got plenty of both to last us for the rest of the trip. Let's get cleaned up now and have a captain's dinner to celebrate the end of this crossing."

Out on deck Zack and Salty had baths, using buckets and buckets of fresh water. Then they went below to the galley, where Zack heated two cans of Salty's favorite, yummy beef stew.

As they finished eating, Zack noticed the wind had begun to blow very hard. He tuned in the boat's radio and received a weather report that warned of a bad storm working its way toward Hawaii. Small boats were advised to head for the nearest port.

"Guess that means us." Zack hurried to lower the sails before they were ripped by the winds. Then he battened down the hatches and stowed loose gear in the ship's lockers.

At dawn, waves began to break over the little boat's bow and wash across her decks.

"We'll be safer down in the cabin. Get below right now," Zack sharply commanded his crew.

Salty scrambled down the companionway. Zack quickly followed and grabbed for the boat's radio.

"MAYDAY! MAYDAY! This is VJ10427, VJ10427, tan-and-white sailboat taking on water," Zack called out to the Coast Guard for help, giving the boat's exact longitude and latitude. "Heavy seas are carrying my boat, with a crew of two, dangerously close to shore."

The Coast Guard answered immediately. They assured Zack that a rescue team would be sent right away, gave the Coast Guard station name and number, and signed off.

"I know you're frightened," Zack told a trembling Salty. "I'm frightened, too, but we've got to hang in there and be brave together."

Back up on deck, waiting for the Coast
Guard, Zack took a firm hold of Salty
and unhooked the lifelines. Now both
sailors were free to swim ashore if the
boat began to sink or capsize before help
arrived.

Suddenly a giant wave crashed down
onto the deck, sweeping Zack and Salty
into the sea!

Salty tumbled over and over through
the foaming surf, bobbing up and down
like a little cork.

Soon waves carried Salty up onto a sandy beach.

Salty was safe now, but where was Zack? He ran back and forth searching frantically for his master. What was that over there? Salty raced toward a dark shape floating in shallow water. It was Zack! Salty grabbed Zack's shirt in his teeth and pulled with all his strength to get Zack out of the water and up onto the sand. Then he barked and barked.

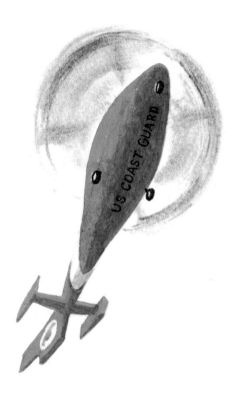

People living nearby heard Salty barking and came running out onto the beach. At the same time a Coast Guard helicopter landed on the shore. They all had come to help the shipwrecked sailors.

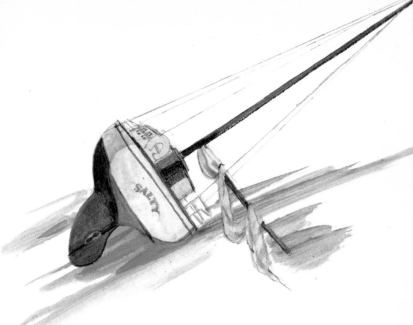

Zack, who had been knocked unconscious when he was swept overboard, came to. He sat up and coughed hard because he'd choked on a lot of water.

"Salty, Salty, where's Salty?" he asked as soon as he could talk.

At the sound of Zack's voice Salty went wild. He whimpered and cried and jumped right into Zack's lap.

Neither Zack nor Salty was badly hurt, just battered by the sea. Their boat, found beached in the next cove, was only slightly damaged.

For the next few days, while Zack and Salty recovered from the shipwreck, their new Hawaiian friends prepared a luau especially for them.

It was a wonderful party. There was a feast of roasted whole pig, raw and cooked fish of every kind, taro leaves stuffed with meat, and a dessert of delicious coconut pudding.

Singers and ukulele players filled the air with soft Hawaiian music. Everyone danced the hula except Salty. He just ran around in crazy circles yelping, having a very good time.

"I wouldn't be here for all this fun if you hadn't pulled me out of the water and barked for help, Salty," Zack said, saluting his dog. "You saved my life. No captain ever had a smarter, more loyal crew."

Zack put a flower lei around Salty's neck, then gave Salty a big hug. "Well done, Old Salt."

Salty stood proudly by his commander's side, a true sailor ready to return to sea.